LOVE LETTER CHRONICLES-BOOK 3

A LOVE LETTER TO YOU

HEALING THROUGH WRITING

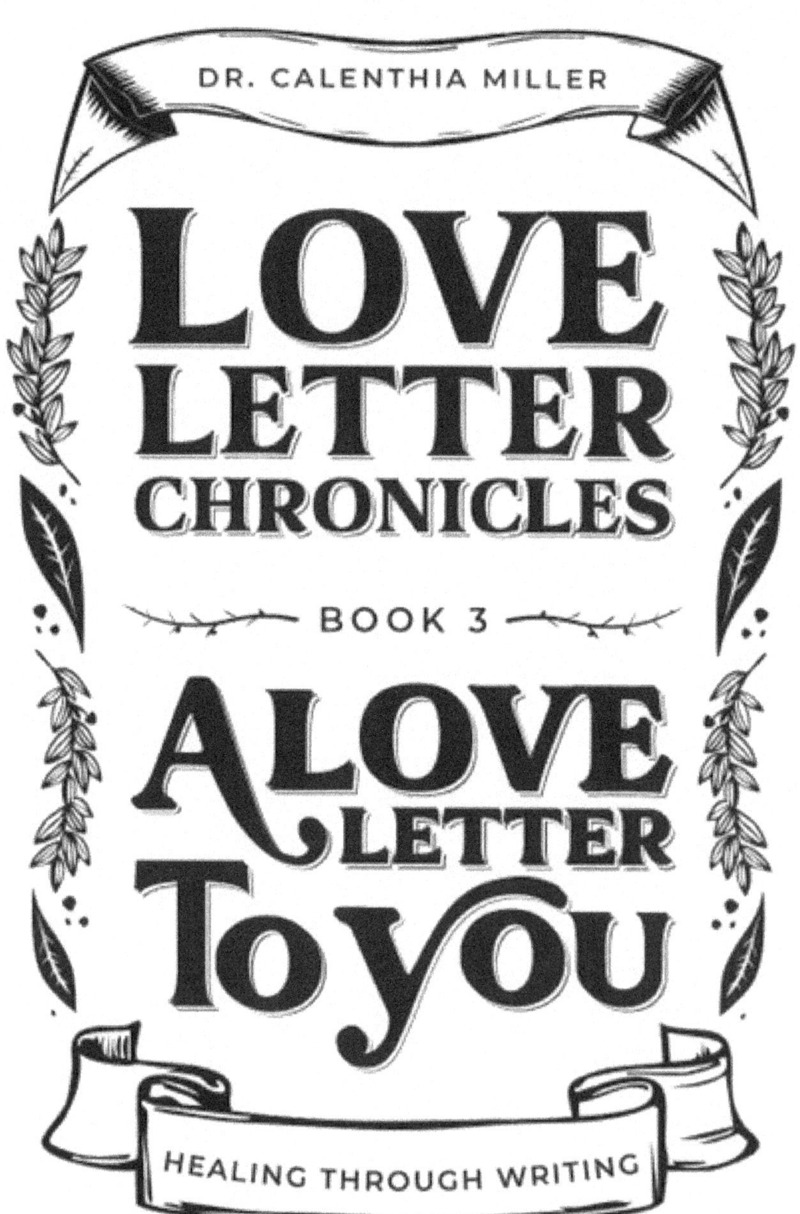

DR. CALENTHIA MILLER
LOVE LETTER CHRONICLES
BOOK 3
A LOVE LETTER TO YOU
HEALING THROUGH WRITING

The Love Letter Chronicles Book 3- A Love Letter to You: Healing Through Writing

Copyright ©2025 By Dr. Calenthia Yvette Miller

For information, contact:

alurepublishingllc@gmail.com

www.alurepublishing.net

ISBN: 979-8-9902920-5-5 (Paperback)

Publication Date: May 21, 2025

DEDICATION

This book is a heartfelt dedication to those navigating through their healing season, a journey filled with challenges and triumphs. It honors individuals bravely confronting their struggles and finding solace in moments of self-discovery and growth. May this work serve as a supportive companion, offering insights and encouragement as you embrace the transformative power of healing.

AUTHOR'S NOTE

This book is a compilation of writings from individuals who have faced setbacks, hardships, or trauma and are on their healing journey. These letters celebrate the transformative power of self-love, personal growth, and happiness, emphasizing the significance of perseverance and self-affirmation. Through their heartfelt expressions, the writers inspire readers to embrace their unique stories and acknowledge the beauty in their life journeys.

Table of Content

INTRODUCTION

Welcome to the third volume of *The Love Letter Chronicles*. In the first two books, *A Love Letter to Me: Creating Conscious Awareness Through Affirmations* and *A Love Letter to Ourselves: An Anthology of Affirmations from Around the World*, we embarked on a journey of self-discovery, self-love, and affirmation. Now, with *A Love Letter to You: Healing Through Writing*, we enter a new chapter—one that explores the depths of trauma, healing, and transformation through the power of writing.

Through these deeply personal narratives, each author shares their unique journey, revealing the profound impact of writing as a healing tool. Their words create a rich tapestry of experiences, providing insight into emotional release, self-discovery, and the therapeutic benefits of self-expression.

Writing can transform pain into strength, uncertainty into clarity, and wounds into wisdom. It enables us to confront our past, embrace our present, and envision a future filled with resilience and hope.

This book explores what healing means—whether through self-reflection, resilience, or external support. It examines the role of trauma in shaping our lives and how overcoming adversity can lead to profound personal growth. These pages serve as a testament to the power of self-affirmation, vulnerability, and the unyielding human spirit.

What Does Trauma Look Like?

Trauma manifests in various internal and external ways. *Emotionally*, it can lead to anxiety, persistent sadness, or a sense of detachment. It can make it difficult to trust others, disrupt relationships, and create feelings of isolation.

Psychologically, trauma often manifests as intrusive thoughts, flashbacks, or nightmares that replay distressing experiences, disrupting daily life. Common symptoms include memory challenges, difficulty concentrating, and emotional numbness.

Physically, it can cause sleep disturbances, changes in appetite, chronic pain, or heightened alertness. Some may turn to unhealthy coping mechanisms, while others may experience persistent restlessness or a sense of being on edge.

Externally, trauma may appear as withdrawal from social interactions, mood fluctuations, or sudden behavioral changes. Recognizing these signs is essential in understanding the lasting impact of trauma and the importance of compassionate support in the healing journey.

What Does it Mean to Heal?

Healing is a deeply personal and transformative process—one that requires patience, self-compassion, and courage. Whether recovering from emotional wounds, personal hardships, or physical trauma, the journey begins by creating a safe space for reflection. This safe space is not solely physical but also emotional and mental. It is the space where you allow yourself to feel, express, and release.

True healing requires acknowledgment—recognizing the pain, naming the emotions, and allowing yourself to process them without fear or shame. It is about embracing your story, not as a burden but as a testament to your strength and resilience. By opening yourself to reflection and self-expression, you begin to shift from merely surviving to truly healing.

A crucial part of this journey is seeking support from trusted friends, family, or professionals who can guide and uplift you. Healing is not meant to be done in isolation; instead, it flourishes in connection and understanding.

Just as a wound requires care to heal, your heart and mind also need nurturing. Establishing a routine that includes self-care, mindfulness, and healthy coping strategies helps you reclaim your peace. With consistent effort and self-commitment, you pave the way for personal transformation and emotional restoration.

The Building Blocks of Healing

Healing is not a one-size-fits-all process; however, there are some foundational steps that can support your journey toward renewal.

1. **Identify the Root Cause:** Understanding the cause of your pain or trauma is the first step toward healing. By identifying the root of your emotions, you can start to address them constructively and meaningfully.

2. **Seek Professional Therapy:** Healing doesn't mean you have to go through it alone. A licensed therapist or counselor can help you process your experiences, develop coping strategies, and provide valuable tools for emotional well-being.

3. **Set Realistic Goals:** Transformation occurs through small, consistent steps. Establish achievable goals that encourage progress, no matter how minor they may appear. Every step forward is a victory.

4. **Embrace Journaling:** Writing is a powerful tool for self-discovery and healing. Pouring your thoughts onto paper allows you to release emotions, reflect on your journey, and track your progress over time. This practice can bring clarity and help you reframe your experiences with a sense of purpose.

5. **Prioritize Self-Care:** Taking care of yourself is not a luxury—it is a necessity. Engage in activities that bring you joy, whether it's reading, exercising, listening to music, or simply resting. Self-care replenishes your spirit and strengthens your resilience.

6. **Practice Meditation and Mindfulness:** Grounding yourself in the present moment can bring immense relief. Practices such as meditation,

deep breathing, or mindful reflection can help calm the mind, reduce stress, and provide a sense of inner peace.

7. **Seek Social and Familiar Support:** Surrounding yourself with supportive individuals who uplift and validate your experiences can be profoundly healing. Whether through friendships, family, or community, connection nurtures strength and reassurance.

The Role of Love in Healing

At the core of healing is love. Love, in its various forms, serves as the foundation for self-affirmation, connection, and growth. It shapes our self-perception and influences our relationships with others.

Love is more than words—it is an action, a commitment, and a daily practice. It is found in moments of kindness, deep conversations, forgiveness, and the courage to be vulnerable. When we integrate love into our lives, we create a path toward wholeness, fulfillment, and lasting transformation.

A Celebration of Healing and Growth

This book is a compelling collection of letters from individuals who have faced adversity, hardship, and trauma yet have discovered strength in their healing journey. Through their words they celebrate self-love, personal growth, and the unbreakable human spirit.

May these stories inspire you to embrace your own journey—to find solace in writing, courage in reflection, and hope in every chapter of your life.

EMBRACE YOUR JOURNEY OF HEALING

DEAR ROYCE

Royce Dixon Sr.

Dear Royce,

Over the years I've had the chance to watch you move and grow into the man I admire. I know it's hard for you to receive compliments, and rarely do you compliment yourself. I have watched you fulfill your dreams that you never thought possible. I have watched you step out in faith and move when God told you to move. You have embraced your inner power and unlocked the gifts placed inside of you.

Now, let me remind you what the Word says:

"I can do all things through Christ who strengthens me" (Phil. 4:13, NKJV).

"He who is in you is greater than he who is in the world" (1 John 4:4).

Why am I telling you these things? Because every so often, you allow others to dictate how you move. You seek out others' approval who may not know what it is you truly need. You give weight to their opinions on a vision that God gave *you*—not them. And you allow their thoughts to influence that vision. I pray you grow more confident in yourself and your abilities. You are a natural at so many things! The Lord would not put you out there to stand all alone without some confidence. And if He is there for you, who can stand against you?

Think about this for a second: You're the CEO of Be Blessed Culture. You have Be Blessed Clothing, photography, and you are a published author of four books (*Hidden Feelings, Blessed While Broken, JoJo's Learning Adventures,* and

Hidden Feelings Revealed: Is There More). A fifth book, *A Rose on the Concrete Court*, will soon be released.

You have done *a lot*, but you have much more to do. Let me remind you that you are carrying a blessing for others, so it is vitally important that you remain locked in and focused on the task ahead. Someone, somewhere, might be watching you to see how you move to overcome.

If all these things are insufficient to keep you pushing forward and going after what you want, I want you to consider your reasons. What you are doing is creating a legacy for the future. You are breaking generational curses and pushing your family forward.

Even after you are gone, your family will have your written works that will serve as a blueprint to remind them that if you can do it, so can they. It will show them what determination and strong belief can do together. It will teach them that when you decrease yourself and make it all about Him, you will see what He can do for you in return.

I will leave you with one final thought: *You matter.* You never have to hide who you are to fit in. You never have to downplay your gift or brag about it to get noticed. Your reward may not come in the form of money; however, you *are* successful. You have been called to do exactly what you are doing, so keep striving and press on. As the older generation used to say, "You're storing timber to build that final home."

Keep growing, learning, and moving forward. Only *you* can stop yourself. You are equipped with everything you need to be successful.

Sincerely yours,

Royce Dixon Sr.

YOU ARE STILL STANDING

Pamela James-Coleman

Today, I take a moment to reflect and realize how far I've come. Remembering everything I experienced as a child, I can see now that it did not break me. What I went through made me stronger and has empowered me to share my experiences with others. I have learned that I can let people know they are not alone on their journey through mental abuse.

So here's a note from me to you:

Dear Pamela,

You did it! I am proud of you and all that you are accomplishing. No one ever called you beautiful or intelligent, no matter how hard you tried to fit in. You may not have found your place among others, but you never gave up.

Don't look back or dwell on the past; your experiences have shaped the person you are meant to be. Growing up in the church, you understand that God will not give you more than you can handle. Look at everything you have overcome. Each fight you've faced has made you stronger. Some challenges would have broken others, but you persisted for your kids and grandmother.

Stand in front of the mirror and see the woman everyone else sees. I want you to meet Pamela James Coleman: mother, grandmother, friend, and boss. Never forget that you are beautiful—inside and out. I know you may not see it, but you are, and I hope one day you will embrace this and see yourself as others see you.

Stay on the path God has laid out for you. Recognize that the work you are doing is helping others. You are fighting a battle many would walk away from, and I am proud of you for your resilience. Never stop believing in yourself and your ability to make a difference.

Signed,

Yourself.

WHISPERED REFLECTIONS

Phyllis Y. Whitley

"If loving self is right,

I don't want to be wrong."

I will not compromise my song.

Hey, beautiful soul,

it's time we have a heart-to-heart.

Do you remember being three,

carrying weights too heavy for tiny hands,

as your sister swung blows

that were never meant for you,

but for the emptiness she felt as the middle child?

Yes, I remember.

The whispers of rejection,

doors shut, family crossing streets to silence my name?

The schoolyard taunts, laughter masking wounds,

seeking refuge in family, only to be met with indifference.

And when my older sister banished me, replacing love with lies,

while I moved from state to state,

searching for the family I never knew?

Yes, I remember.

And then came love—

Through my mother and stepfather's eyes

Drowned in bottles,

slurred in screams—

a battlefield, not a home.

It taught me survival, not surrender.

When innocence was not lost,

but stolen?

By hands that had no right,

in a world that only whispered my pain?

Yes, I remember.

The heartbreak of marrying a prince I never knew existed,

his mother deemed me unworthy.

While I ran from his love,

he found another who embraced him with ease.

Once again, I shut love out my door,

afraid to be known, afraid to be seen.

Yes, I remember.

The rejection—

family feasts full, yet my name missing.

Arms meant to hold me stayed folded.

Fleeing New York,

not chasing dreams,

but escaping a mother who found solace in a bottle.

Avoiding battles, she refused to fight.

The shame. The silence. The world's cold shoulder.

Yes, I remember.

Do you remember the weight of being a mother?

Holding a baby girl,

terrified that love

was a language you never learned?

Yes, I remember.

When God found me,

when the church that was supposed to heal me

only mirrored the brokenness

I was trying to escape—

Yes, I do remember.

And then cancer came,

knocking at my door,

uninvited, unwanted, unrelenting.

Carrying it alone,

whispering through the pain?

Your daughter, your anchor,

whispering, sharing the load—

and you did.

And for a moment, family arrived,

only to vanish like a mist

when they realized you wouldn't die.

Yes, I remember.

The final farewell,

love given where others would not.

And when my mother's funeral ended,

their hands withdrew once more.

Yes, I remember.

The one who never left?

Who prayed, stood, and carried you through?

Your daughter—unshaken, unwavering.

The degrees earned, the home built and lost,

bankruptcy, and the rise from the ashes.

Do you remember pushing love away,

believing solitude was safer

than being traumatized again?

Yes, I remember.

The moment you chose you?

When you realized

the whispers within were not broken,

but a calling to consciousness?

When you knew

you were never alone—

because God had never left?

The first book.

The first business.

The lives touched.

Forgiving—not for them, but for you.

Letting go, stepping fully into your promised land.

The most crucial choice of all?

The moment you finally loved yourself—

fully, freely, fiercely—

and accepted God as your family,

without apology,

without hesitation,

without fear?

Yes, I remember.

And that, my dear,

is the only memory that matters now.

With love,

Me.

I CANNOT DO THIS WITHOUT YOU, GOD

Ann Dyson

As I grew up, my eyes captured many things, and my ears heard many sounds. Yet, I often overlooked certain things, perhaps due to the love that enveloped me. I heard and didn't hear because of the love, affection, and care surrounding me while growing up with my siblings—my six plus one.

There were instances of physical and mental abuse, both good and bad days, experiences of plenty and others of scarcity, hurt, control, negative influences, black-and-white issues, disappointments, shattered dreams, and choices made by others that I had no say in. Through it all, God protected me. The "six plus one" refers to my dad having a child outside of his marriage to my mom, a child we later learned about and welcomed into our hearts.

My mom, sister, and brothers eventually stood up, declaring no more control or harm toward our mother. We stood firm in the name of Jesus, seeking God's help. My mom was a jewel, filled with God's spirit, radiating love in every direction. Every Sunday, we gathered as a family after church, and her grace and mercy shone through her character like the polish on a new pair of church shoes.

My mom prayed that she would see me grow into womanhood. Although I had graduated high school when she left this world, I was still young, and that experience has continued to impact me profoundly. I don't limit my prayers; I let the Holy Spirit guide me and never stop connecting with God.

My sister was an impressive woman of God who developed into an influential and direct person. My mom passed away shortly before my sister survived a brutal attack by her husband, who had attacked her and left her for dead while attempting to come after me. Thanks to God, my sister survived the ordeal. At times, she questioned her purpose in life beyond caring for older adults and babysitting, but God had granted her the gifts of prophecy and discernment.

My sister could often tell you things you had already done or considered doing, making you laugh with the realization that she was right. Her God-given gift was mighty. I would spend hours discussing spiritual matters with my mom while seeking my sister's company to walk, talk, or ride with me because I valued her presence.

Years later, after cheating death, my sister passed away from an illness, leaving me feeling alone in this world once again. The pain of losing my mother and then my sister hurt me deeply. To emulate my mom, as the old blues song says, is to be awesome, and to imitate my sister is to be great. While my mom and sister were alive, they brought joy to everything.

Although I have their spiritual love, protection, compassion, and comfort, I deeply miss the physical touch, hug, and conversation. One lesson they taught me was the path to Jesus, which I chose to follow. It was the missing piece I had been seeking. Jesus had always been there, but I told myself I could not do life on my own during certain times. I had to find strength in Jesus by realizing that, as the Scripture says in John 16:33, "These things I have spoken to you, that in me you may have peace."

I have been married for what feels like a lifetime—over forty years. My relationship has grown moment by moment and year by year. My husband and I have raised three exceptional children, who are now married with their own families. God has never once failed me. I am grateful for the joy of watching our children grow through Christ Jesus; it has been both wonderful and, at times, heartbreaking. But look at God! It was when I connected with Him that I found understanding amid all the people who left me, the friendships that faded, and the disappointments of life: sickness, anxiety, hurt, and loneliness.

Life continued, and I learned to take it one moment at a time. My youngest daughter was delivered from depression, my sister passed away, my home burned down, and I had a pacemaker placed in my heart and later removed due to an infection. I underwent knee replacement surgery, and my husband was healed from cancer and survived a terrible accident that broke both femur bones.

They say that when it rains, it pours. But those moments define you, and it's how you handle them that truly matter.

After my pacemaker was removed, I still woke up every morning saying to God, "I am still here, thankful, and trusting you with my life."

While others might complain about the simplest things, I am grateful for life. *Thank you, God.* He sees the bigger plan. I realized I could not live life by myself. Honestly, I cannot. This was one of God's bigger plans: I would not die prematurely and would finish my course no matter how tired I became. I will overcome and mount up with wings like eagles.

Isaiah 40:31 reads, "But those who wait on the Lord shall renew their strength; they shall mount up with wings like eagles, they shall run and not be weary, they shall walk and not faint."

When you feel death coming for you, you begin to wonder *How do I tell my loved ones I'm not going to make it?* Then God comes in closer and heals what is broken—my last knee surgery. At the time my husband was at home with two broken legs. But after the surgery, everything went well.

Deep down, I am once again trying to explain. My soul felt like it had a leak. I stood up with assistance, taking a test to go home. As I sat in a wheelchair in the hospital hallway, attempting to hold my head up, the devil tried to take me down. But God was not ready for me yet. *God, I cannot do this alone!*

When I awoke, I had asked all the staff surrounding me how my daughter was. They had laughed about that being my first concern after I had just woken up from a near-death experience. *Thank you, Father, for loving me and showing me how to love me and my family completely.* You love me enough to use the hospital staff to revive me, but you, my Father, gave the final touch and breathed life into my body once again. *I cannot do it by myself.*

You, my big brother, who always has my back, and the Holy Spirit, my counselor. You will face trials and tribulations but must take ownership of your courage and faith. As a woman, I have overcome the world. It's easy to read about it but much more challenging to put into action. I thank God for the Holy Spirit, grace, and the opportunity to learn from my experiences. To love myself was to learn how to love you all first.

As my brother says, "Do that thing."

And that thing is called love!

FINDING POWER IN THE GLASS BOX

Ta'Jah Cloyd

Traveling down this foggy road, performing the world's longest
monologue.

Caught up in life illusions, distorted vision—

the diagnosis for the problems in my sight.

Prognosis: Clouded judgment. Lack of discernment. Constant despair.

And these clouds don't come with nines, like the life path in God's original
design.

No purpose, no passion. Loss and misfortune. Is this my reality?

Robot voice: Turning on survival mode. Autopilot. I'm no longer in
control.

Drifting further from the end goal. Repeating toxic cycles. Taking
high-risk bets.

Not the bliss I envisioned.

Is it my insecurities—mommy or daddy issues?

Oh, and don't forget that childhood trauma, too.

Google search: How to create an attached avoidant.

I am in need of deep inner child healing,

remembering why I picked up this pen to begin with.

An emotionally unavailable mother—no space for a child's voice to be
heard.

An absent, imprisoned father—no place for a daughter to be loved.

Mistaking sexual abuse for the love and validation I craved.

I wonder . . . Would things be different if she weren't dismissive?

If I had felt forehead kisses?

My silent trauma crept into my teenage years, making the journey
rougher.

Overindulgence in sex and drugs, constant heartbreak—

each wound made me tougher.

I built a hard exterior, masking myself in glass.

Lost my authenticity in the struggle of imposter syndrome,

Found it again in the reflections of my imperfections.

Villain origin story in the making. Unwilling to compromise.

Self-sabotaging my marriage—the catalyst of my demise.

Freshly single, newfound independence, two babies in my arms.

The pressure building—to become a better me.

They deserve a mother who is more than her depression,

More than her PTSD.

Trying to understand the roots of my self-destruction.

Not to my surprise—it's fear.

Fear that lingers in the loneliest parts of me.

But my spirit is calling for change, whispering:

"What are you willing to exchange for the peace you seek?"

Autopilot off.

Self-isolation leads to self-reflection.

My thoughts race as I face my truth.

Learning to accept accountability for the life I lead.

No longer a victim—finally, I see.

Through shadow work, through breaking generational curses,

I can create a new reality.

Planting a new seed—confidence, faith, and belief.

Becoming everything five-year-old me once dreamed of.

Thank you, Glass Box, for once keeping me safe.

But now, I am ready to build something new.

Not a box unshattered.

But a home. One with a door,

Where I am free.

—Moon thoughts with Ta'Jah C.

HEY YOU, YEAH YOU!

Raquel Wells-Williams

So, I see that you are feeling some kinda way.

I don't know why, because you are enough—

Period.

I know I've ignored you for quite some time, but it was really unintentional!

Life Happened!

You know—the husband, the kids, grandkids, work, church . . . the usual.

This is easy for me to write, but it may be hard for you to accept.

First, stop thinking about the shoulda, coulda, woulda!

Just *be*.

Be glad that you are on this side to even see it.

Whatever "it" is, you are here now.

Second, remember the last time I told you to put on some red lipstick and your red pumps and go be *fierce*? I meant that!

Third, you ready?

Uninvite yourself to the parties, accept that second chin, and keep using those filters!

Let them titties swang and bang in that Walmart bra! Keep wearing those black tights and oversized T-shirts!

Remember—back in the day, Granny wore a moo moo, and Granddaddy still came home every night!

This letter may be hard to take seriously because it's saying that it's okay to accept the imperfections. But seriously . . .

I like you—I think I may even love you!

I know you think you're sexy! I see the way you look at yourself when you walk past a mirror. I notice how you pull that visor down, pretending to check your nose, girl.

Who do you think you're fooling? You know you ROCK!

You are the *sugar*, the *honey*, the *ice*, and the *tea*!

Love always,

Raquel

IGNITE THE FIRE WITHIN

Dr. Calenthia Y. Miller

My inner light has not merely flickered timidly in the shadows; there have been remarkable moments when it has shone with intensity, illuminating the darkness that often feels overwhelming and oppressive. During these times, I have felt a sense of empowerment, as if my essence could push back against despair and uncertainty. I have realized how easily doubt can seep into my thoughts, casting a veil over clarity and making every decision seem fraught with ambiguity.

The struggle against this doubt is a constant battle, reminding me of the fragility of confidence and the strength of perseverance. Yet, when my light shone, it brought clarity and enveloped me like a warm embrace, reassuring me that I was not alone and that brighter days were possible.

As I immersed myself in reflection, gazing back at the tapestry of the past year, I was struck by the incredible journey of growth and transformation I had undertaken. Each moment became a stepping stone, leading me to new heights. Throughout this voyage, I discovered profound insights about Calenthia, unearthing layers of understanding that enriched my experiences and shaped my perspective.

My story is still being written, and I pray that as each page turns, readers will see that I am a work in progress and that God is tirelessly working *for* me, *with* me, and *through* me. Today, I'm isolating myself to protect my peace. And before you ask, I'm not running away or hiding; I'm building the strength to keep going in this race. So be encouraged as your light shines brightly within.

Dr. C.

A BRIGHTER DAY IS COMING!

Elogeia Hadley

I have been fighting for as long as I can remember—fighting people and situations. As a child I was often labeled "fearless." I possessed a keen awareness of the world around me, absorbing everything. I enjoyed spending time with elders, listening to their stories and learning valuable skills like cooking, sewing, and singing. Fortunately, I had a grandmother and aunts who encouraged me to be myself, even when children were expected to be seen and not heard.

My mother constantly reminded me of my intelligence and instilled in me the importance of expressing myself and standing up for my beliefs. I learned so much during those formative years. However, one crucial lesson that no one taught me was managing stress and finding happiness in life and within myself. I now understand why—my family, like many others in our community, was often in survival mode, facing a seemingly endless storm.

It was not until I turned forty, a few years after my son was born, that I began to teach myself how to navigate the chaos. I realized I had been living with depression for years, often consumed by worries about my health and how I looked. As the parent of an autistic child, I had no choice but to prioritize my well-being and practice self-care. Seeking out a therapist was a pivotal step toward healing. I began to focus more on myself and less on the external pressures of the world around me.

Every day remains a challenge, and I constantly engage in self-encouragement, understanding the importance of self-preservation in this fight for survival. I returned to the things that brought me joy, particularly writing. This form of expression became my refuge; I would often be so deeply engaged in my writing that I would lose track of time, only realizing how much time had passed when the day had already gone. In those moments, I rediscovered the childlike wonder I had almost forgotten. Reflecting on memories of pop-up books and scratch-and-sniff stickers reminded me of the joy that life can offer.

I promised to live each moment as if it were my last. Life is a precious journey, and I am grateful for every experience. Seeing so many people burdened by regrets and unable to pursue their passions pains me. I often joke around to lighten the mood, but I feel their struggles deeply. I find profound joy in these writing moments, a gentle reminder that tomorrow holds hope and the promise of better days. I cherish my life experiences, embrace the journey ahead, and always remember that a brighter day is coming.

STRENGTH IN HEALING ONE ANOTHER

Marc "Black Cyrano" Beausejour

Take a look into my eyes, my sister; I can see that you're distressed.

Your relationship's a mess; you've regressed in your faith with no rest,

wishing for success, but it's so elusive to the point that you can't stand.

You find yourself depending on a new man who can never understand

why you're so indecisive, changing hands within the next glance,

trying to take a stance, but you fall victim to deception and faux romance.

He spurns you the next day and leaves you beggin' for one more chance.

He's a man who's unable to trust, so led by his lust, he covets another.

You harbor hatred within; convinced that love never wins, you seek a
lover.

A brother who has shared from the same cup of heartbreak and early pain.

Chained by the nation's excess, repressed by past regrets, hard falls like
rain.

He was shot, beaten, strangled, hung; his hope and potential was dead.

It's been said there was a ransom on his head, for he was believed to be internally led

by a force that has driven him clear across the thoughts and perception of men.

Many a tale has been written about this fellow, who would someday rise again,

to take his place among those who were revered in life and cemented in history.

But why the lady and young man decide to join forces against the system's a mystery.

A world ravaged by war, split across the landscape by color, and divided by politicians.

They take constant punishment from fighting this battle, this ultimate war of attrition.

We see you in poor conditions, despite your efforts to hide your face in anger and shame.

It's hard to explain, but you find yourself living tied up, bound and locked in a frame,

bearing your name, but this world is beyond offensive and impervious to innovation.

The thought or the contemplation that the life you live is acceptable brings up conviction.

I beseech you to let this letter express these words, and don't ever think to hesitate, but rather concentrate on inner peace and the sanctimonious departure from self-hate.

For the healing that you both seek is within the journey of life that we all travel through.

Although I can't see who reads this letter, for the eyes that fall upon these words—this is for you.

Marc "Black Cyrano" Beausejour

A LOVE LETTER TO THE WORLD

Shenitha Finesse Anniece

The last love letter I wrote was to myself, and this love letter will be to the world.

There have been a few significant events: California's and Canada's wildfires; the presidential election; the Washington, D.C., midair collision between an American Airlines passenger jet and a U.S. Army Black Hawk helicopter, where all sixty-seven individuals aboard both aircraft perished; the Seattle airport collision between a Japan Airlines plane and a Delta Airlines plane; and the Philadelphia air ambulance crash, to name a few. Not to mention, Tammera L. Holmes, someone I was honored to meet and hoping to one day call a friend in aviation, lost her life to an internal sickness.

These events highlight the ongoing challenges posed by natural disasters and the critical importance of aviation safety measures—and I have the audacity to be traveling several times throughout this new year.

And beyond these public events, as I transition from 2024 into 2025, I find myself facing personal challenges I never could have imagined. Something deep and heavy has hit close to home—real-life trafficking and a narcissistic situation have altered the course of my life and the decisions that I now make as an individual, parent, daughter, and companion. I have to navigate the daily concern of seeing my daughters go to school with fear and not knowing what derogatory names they will be called or who will target them next. It's disheartening to realize that despite the school's supposed zero-tolerance policy on bullying, the reality feels far from that promise—leaving us to face each day with uncertainty and distress.

Yet, through the shadows, I see the light midway through this tunnel. It has sparked within me the urge to write a fiction book based on my recent experiences, in which all four of my daughters will co-author. This moment of raw truth and clarity leads me to share the following words:

Dear World,

I may not know all of you, but it feels as though we are collectively facing trials that test our hearts and our spirits. We have seen disasters that rip through our homes and lives lost to events that may or may not be due to our own decisions. We have witnessed pain, heartbreak, and fear, and we have stood at the edge of uncertainty, wondering how to heal—some of whom have made permanent decisions based on temporary situations. Yet, even amid chaos, there remains something . . . beautiful. There remains the resilience of the human spirit, the strength that rises from the ashes, and the quiet love that persists in the most unlikely of places.

I write this letter not as an observer but as someone who has also felt the weight of this world and, in doing so, discovered a deep and profound love for all it holds. I have learned that even in our deepest despair, grace can be found in the smallest moments of connection. We heal together when we listen to one another's stories, write our stories, and extend our hands and hearts.

I know that the road ahead will not always be easy. We will face personal and collective challenges, but I believe that true love, forgiveness, and amplified communication are the keys to overcoming them. Love for ourselves, our neighbors, our passions, and the journeys we each must walk. There is nothing that can extinguish the power of love for one another once it is awakened within us.

So, to the world, I offer my love, my gratitude, my forgiveness, my hope, my transparency, and my boundaries. *Hope* that we may find peace even in the storm. *Hope* that we may rebuild and, in doing so, remember the beauty in the brokenness. *Hope* that we will stand side by side in times of tragedy and joy because together, we are unstoppable. Together, we can rise.

With love, always and forever,

DEAR YOU

Shartia "Love" Jones

Dear You,

It can take a lifetime to truly grasp Love's depths, meaning, and true elements. Many ask why I believe in Love so intensely. The answer is simple: I know what it feels like to be without it, to feel unloved, broken, misused, and rejected. I've cared for those who have left me. I've smiled through pain and masked heartache with the only strength I had left. The beautiful part of my story is that I also know what it means to find Love, embrace Love, and let Love transform me from the inside out.

See, I always knew God gave me Love automatically. However, I didn't realize that I had to learn how to receive it. Loving others is great. However, this love is compromised when we try to give it away before fully embracing it for ourselves. We can't successfully offer what we don't have. When this happens, that effort of Love may be abused and we can feel drained from the process. This is why embracing Love for yourself is imperative.

"Loving yourself" is not just a cliché or catchy phrase, it's real and intentional work. It requires quiet moments, prayer, patience, and daily habits that feed your spirit. Speaking life over yourself, carving out time for you, and forgiving yourself are examples of this work. Showing up for yourself is a great representation of Love.

Love is a powerful force. It transforms hate, heals brokenness, and can resurrect what feels lost. Be that as it may, what happens when Love is neglected, misunderstood, or when pain feels more powerful than Love? Sometimes, "Love" can feel distant or even cruel. I can recall searching for it only to find emptiness, coupled with loveless experiences. Sitting with my pain was my key to growth and healing. This healing starts when we stop running and start reflecting.

There was a defining moment on my journey as warm tears streamed down my face and crawled down my lips. I also felt a tingly... Yet, a comforting revelation! I'd realized Love had been within me all along, and I didn't need anyone to validate a Love that already had God's stamp on it! I just had to welcome this healing journey and do the work.

That's what I call *the mirror effect.* When we learn to love ourselves and look in the mirror to reflect, we stop expecting fragments of masked Love from others. We also stop relying on validation from others to prove we're enough. If we don't know how to Love ourselves, how will we know what real Love looks sounds or feels like? Prioritizing yourself is key. You are worth the discovery and the care.

Love is an action word. It is a choice and must be practiced. I often think about those science fair projects with the plants. Some were nurtured and others were neglected. The plants that didn't grow weren't stalled because they were incapable of growth. They died because they were deprived of what was necessary for their survival. The same is true for us.

We need Love to survive. We can pretend we don't. However, deep down, we all want to Love and be Loved. Oftentimes, fear, doubt, and past wounds cause us to rebel against Love. In that space, we deny ourselves the very thing that gives life meaning, hope and purpose.

I'm not perfect. However, I Love deeply and refuse to give up on Love. I've learned that when you choose Love, it chooses you back! Yes, I've been told my Love was "too much." Yet, I will never apologize for how I Love. My empathy, care and ability to see others is a gift. It is my personal superpower. On this journey, you'll learn that everyone won't be able to receive your Love, and that's okay. To those of you who Love fiercely, keep Loving and remember to set boundaries. Protect your heart while still showing up in your truth. Your Love is unique, and the right people will cherish and honor it.

Love is not just a feeling. It's a key. A balm. A divine gift. If God didn't Love me, I wouldn't be here writing this. Love literally saved me from me. I had a friend ask me, what good is a gift if you never unwrap it?! He was right! Since then, I vowed to keep unraveling my gift(s), and hope you do the same. Love is a beautiful catalyst for change. You have the power to Love and be Loved. Just remember to start with you. You are worth the win!

Love is 1 Corinthians 13:4.

Love is also the greatest Fruit of the Spirit, and fruit grows from a seed when it's nurtured right.

I'll leave you with these words my Pastor always says to us:

"I love you, and there ain't nothing you can do about it."

Con Amor Siempre,

Shartia "Love" Jones

It's my namesake and my heart's passion.

Lead with heart, and you'll always find your path. #LoveWins

A LETTER TO TORRIE

Torrie Q. Jones

Dear Torrie,

This letter is only for you. I am not talking to the mother in you, the career-driven girl, or the book author. I am just talking to Torrie. So, sit and listen, and you might learn something.

First, you are not a superwoman, and it's not your fault. It's not your fault that the people you believed were close to you betrayed you. It's not your fault for choosing people who didn't choose you. It's not your fault that your parents never had the chance to live. It's not your responsibility to save others from themselves. It's not your job to serve or save the world. However, it is your obligation to save yourself from procrastination, emotional turmoil, and financial distress.

You are strong, resilient, ambitious, beautiful, loved, and appreciated. You are right (most of the time). Lol. Also, remember that you are soft, sensitive, emotional, and short. *Smile.* You do not have to do it all. It's okay to be vulnerable and ask for help.

The beautiful woman you've become is awe-inspiring. Who would have thought this is the life you've built? Don't worry about the past. Much of it wasn't your fault. It's okay to take responsibility for the negative things you're willing to acknowledge, but stop beating yourself up!

It happened. It's done. You are no longer that person. You are not in those situations or environments anymore. Let it go! Move forward. Keep seeking spiritual guidance. God and your ancestors have been watching over and protecting you all this time. Keep believing that!

Remember, there is nothing wrong with you. Don't let what you're going through isolate you. Reach out to your support resources and be honest about your mental and physical well-being. Many people are willing to help if you let them. Make your plans, stick to them, be mindful of your spending, and keep striving for what you want. Solidifying those plans will make them come true. Get out of that funk and do it!

Love always and forever,

Torrie Q. Jones

YOUR JOURNEY STARTS WITH YOU!

YOUR LETTER TO YOU

Begin Your Healing Letter

Now that you've explored the foundations of healing through the journey of our esteemed authors, it's time to take an active step forward. Writing your own letter can be a profound and cathartic experience. It allows you to express your pain, acknowledge your progress, and speak words of love and encouragement to yourself. Find a quiet space, take a deep breath, and begin with these prompts:

Dear Me,

What do you need to hear right now? What words of kindness, hope, or reassurance can you offer yourself?

I release . . .

What burdens or past experiences are you prepared to let go of?

I choose . . .

What positive changes and affirmations do you wish to embrace as you move forward?

Words of Encouragement

Here are some inspirational quotes to guide you as you write your letter:

The wound is the place where the Light enters you. —Rumi

Healing may not be so much about getting better, as about letting go of everything that isn't you . . . and becoming who you are. — Rachel Naomi Remen

You don't have to control your thoughts. You just have to stop letting them control you. — Dan Millman

Your past does not define you. Your healing, your growth, and your resilience do. — Anonymous

Your healing journey is uniquely yours, but you are never alone. Let your words be your guide and may this letter to yourself be the first step toward profound healing and transformation.

Your journey of healing begins today.

Your Love Letter To You

SPECIAL THANKS

ROYCE DIXON SR.

PAMELA JAMES COLEMAN

PHYLLIS Y. WHITLEY

ANN DYSON

TA'JAH CLOYD

RAQUEL WELLS-WILLIAMS

DR. CALENTHIA Y. MILLER

ELOGEIA HADLEY

MARC "BLACK CYRANO" BEAUSEJOUR

SHENITHA FINESSE ANNIECE

SHARTIA "LOVE" JONES

TORRIE Q. JONES

*In this season, as you walk in your purpose,
remember that each step you take must match
the words you speak.*

Dr. C.

www.ingramcontent.com/pod-product-compliance
Lightning Source LLC
Chambersburg PA
CBHW040914010826
48978CB00013BB/1285